BENEDICT BLATHWAYT

The Sticker Atlas of Scotland

Contents

Scotland

If you looked down on Scotland from a great height, this is what you might see.

The outline of Scotland has always been shaped by rising and falling sea levels and eroded by wind, water and ice.

The lower, greener areas of the country provide rich soil for crops and grazing. To the north and west are rugged mountains, deep lochs and glens carved out by the glaciers of past Ice Ages.

SHETLAND ISLANDS

ORKNEY ISLANDS

PENTLAND FIRTH

NORTH SEA

OUTER HEBRIDES

THE MINCH

NORTH-WEST HIGHLANDS

MORAY FIRTH

GREAT GLEN

CAIRNGORM MOUNTAINS

GRAMPIAN MOUNTAINS

INNER HEBRIDES

ATLANTIC OCEAN

TROSSACHS

FIRTH OF FORTH

KINTYRE

SOUTHERN UPLANDS

SCOTTISH BORDERS

FIRTH OF CLYDE

ENGLAND

NORTH

WEST

EAST

SOUTH

| 0 | 20 | 40 | 60 | 80 kilometres |

| 0 | 10 | 20 | 30 | 40 | 50 miles |

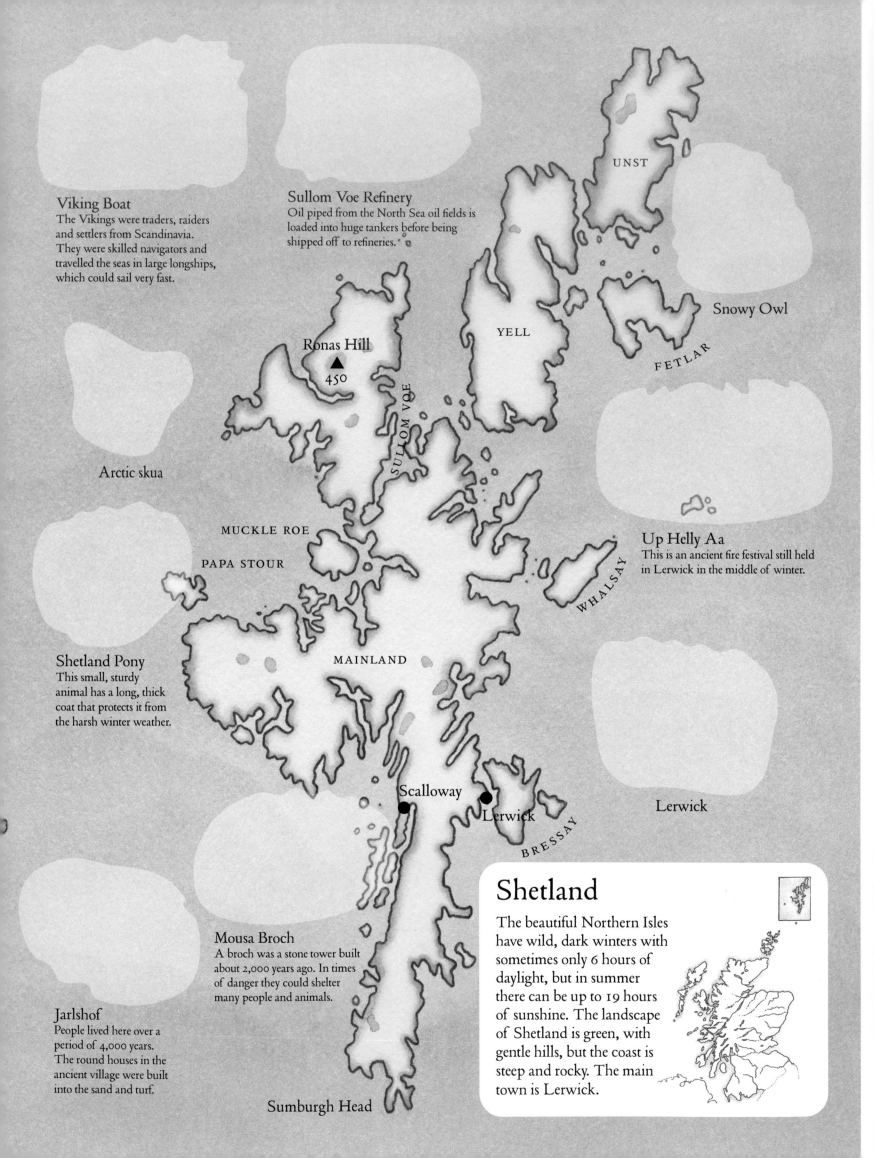

Viking Boat
The Vikings were traders, raiders and settlers from Scandinavia. They were skilled navigators and travelled the seas in large longships, which could sail very fast.

Sullom Voe Refinery
Oil piped from the North Sea oil fields is loaded into huge tankers before being shipped off to refineries.

Arctic skua

Ronas Hill
▲
450

UNST

YELL

Snowy Owl

FETLAR

SULLOM VOE

MUCKLE ROE

PAPA STOUR

WHALSAY

Up Helly Aa
This is an ancient fire festival still held in Lerwick in the middle of winter.

Shetland Pony
This small, sturdy animal has a long, thick coat that protects it from the harsh winter weather.

MAINLAND

Scalloway

Lerwick

BRESSAY

Lerwick

Mousa Broch
A broch was a stone tower built about 2,000 years ago. In times of danger they could shelter many people and animals.

Jarlshof
People lived here over a period of 4,000 years. The round houses in the ancient village were built into the sand and turf.

Sumburgh Head

Shetland

The beautiful Northern Isles have wild, dark winters with sometimes only 6 hours of daylight, but in summer there can be up to 19 hours of sunshine. The landscape of Shetland is green, with gentle hills, but the coast is steep and rocky. The main town is Lerwick.

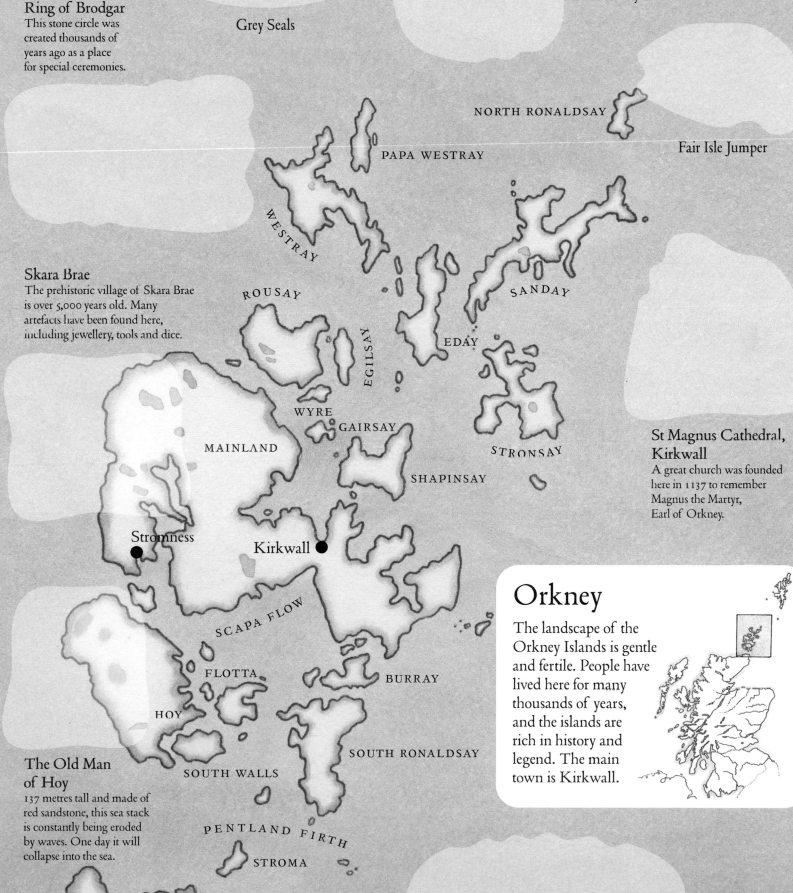

Ring of Brodgar
This stone circle was created thousands of years ago as a place for special ceremonies.

Grey Seals

North Ronaldsay Beacon
There has been a lighthouse here since 1789. The island has its own ancient breed of sheep who live almost entirely on seaweed.

FAIR ISLE

NORTH RONALDSAY

PAPA WESTRAY

Fair Isle Jumper

WESTRAY

Skara Brae
The prehistoric village of Skara Brae is over 5,000 years old. Many artefacts have been found here, including jewellery, tools and dice.

ROUSAY

SANDAY

EDAY

EGILSAY

WYRE

GAIRSAY

MAINLAND

STRONSAY

SHAPINSAY

St Magnus Cathedral, Kirkwall
A great church was founded here in 1137 to remember Magnus the Martyr, Earl of Orkney.

Stromness

Kirkwall

SCAPA FLOW

FLOTTA

BURRAY

HOY

Orkney

The landscape of the Orkney Islands is gentle and fertile. People have lived here for many thousands of years, and the islands are rich in history and legend. The main town is Kirkwall.

SOUTH RONALDSAY

The Old Man of Hoy
137 metres tall and made of red sandstone, this sea stack is constantly being eroded by waves. One day it will collapse into the sea.

SOUTH WALLS

PENTLAND FIRTH

STROMA

John O'Groats

Ferry to Orkney

Cape Wrath

Aurora Borealis
Also called the Northern Lights, this beautiful display of colours in the night sky is created by 'winds' of solar energy high up in the earth's atmosphere.

Sandwood Bay

Great Stack of Handa
Thousands of birds, especially puffins, razorbills and guillemots, make their nests on steep cliffs here.

● Kinlochbervie

Tongue ●

Ben Hope
▲
927

HANDA ISLAND

Foinaven
▲
908

● Scourie

Ardvreck
Castle

Altnahara ●

Great Northern Diver

Ben
Kilbre
▲
959

Quinag
▲
809

LOCH ASSYNT

Ferry to Stornoway

● Lochinver

Ben More Assynt
▲
998

LOCH SHIN

Suilven
▲
732

Suilven
The three peaks of Suilven rise from wild, lonely moorland. The Gaelic name for the highest is Caisteal Liath or 'Grey Castle'.

Lairg ●

SUMMER
ISLES

RIVER OYKEL

RIVER SHIN

Summer Isles

LOCH BROOM

● Ullapool

An Teallach
▲
1062

Rock
Climbing

Heather

Ben Dearg
▲
1081

Poolewe ●

● Gairloch

Slioch
▲
981

Sgurr Mor
▲
1109

Ben Wyviss
▲
1045

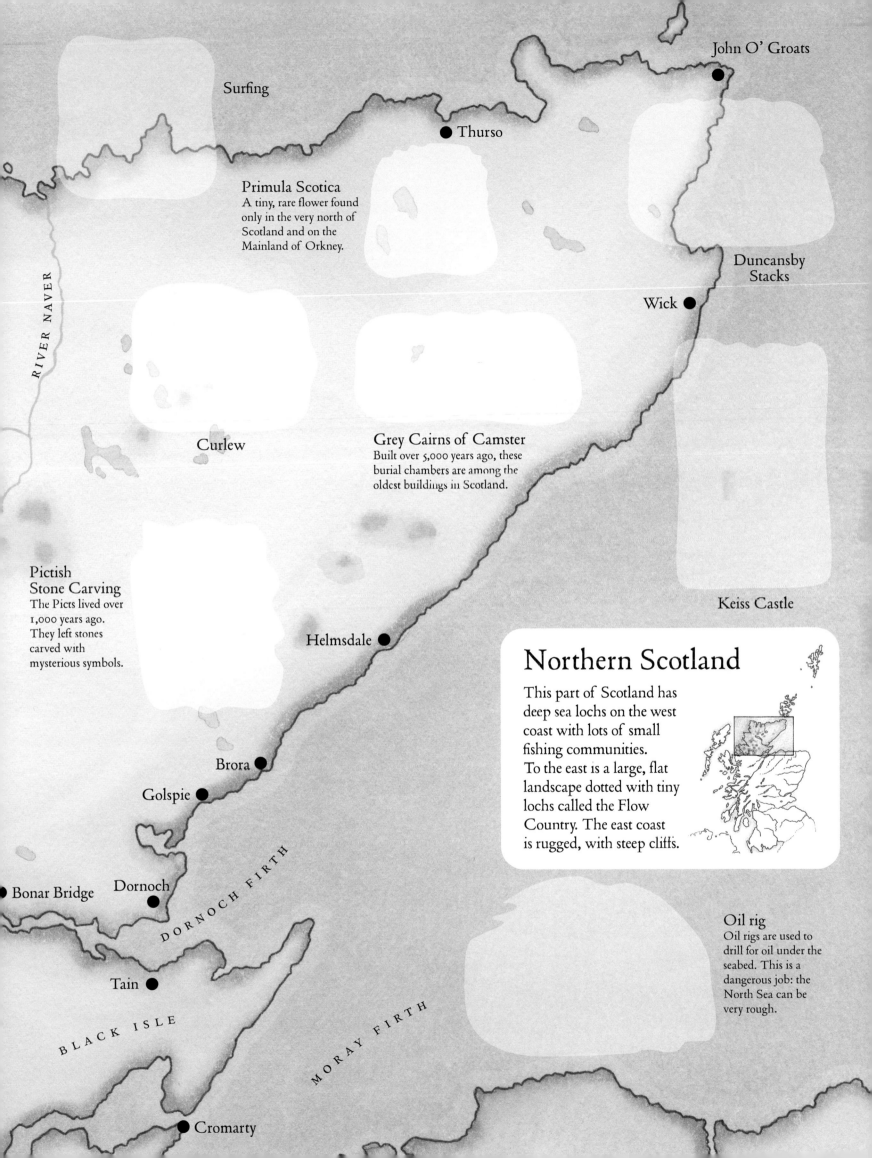

Surfing

John O' Groats

● Thurso

Primula Scotica
A tiny, rare flower found
only in the very north of
Scotland and on the
Mainland of Orkney.

Duncansby
Stacks

Wick ●

RIVER NAVER

Curlew

Grey Cairns of Camster
Built over 5,000 years ago, these
burial chambers are among the
oldest buildings in Scotland.

Pictish
Stone Carving
The Picts lived over
1,000 years ago.
They left stones
carved with
mysterious symbols.

Keiss Castle

Helmsdale ●

Northern Scotland

This part of Scotland has
deep sea lochs on the west
coast with lots of small
fishing communities.
To the east is a large, flat
landscape dotted with tiny
lochs called the Flow
Country. The east coast
is rugged, with steep cliffs.

Brora ●

Golspie ●

● Bonar Bridge

Dornoch
●

DORNOCH FIRTH

Oil rig
Oil rigs are used to
drill for oil under the
seabed. This is a
dangerous job: the
North Sea can be
very rough.

Tain ●

BLACK ISLE

MORAY FIRTH

● Cromarty

MORAY FIRTH

Lossiemouth

Elgin

Dolphins
The Moray Firth is home
to a number of different
kinds of dolphin. You
can see them up close on
special boat trips.

Nairn

Inverness

Urquhart Castle

Battle of Culloden
Bonnie Prince Charlie and his Jacobite supporters
were defeated here in 1746, ending the prince's dream
of becoming King of Great Britain and Ireland.

Grantown-on-Spey

LOCH NESS

Osprey
Loch Garten is one of the
best places in Scotland to
spot the osprey, a rare bird of
prey that catches fish.

RIVER SPEY

Aviemore

Cairn Gorm
▲
1245

Whisky
There are many whisky
distilleries in this part
of Scotland.

Loch Ness Monster
Stories about a mysterious
monster living deep in the
loch have been told for over
1,000 years.

Carn Ban
▲
941

Ben Macdhui
▲
1309

Mountain Hare
As winter approaches, the
mountain hare grows a
white coat. Predators like
the golden eagle are less
likely to see it against the
snow.

Skiing

Braemar ● Lochna
▲
1154

Dalwhinnie

Gentian
The snow
gentian is a
rare mountain
plant.

LOCH ERICHT

Ben Alder
▲
1145

Reindeer

Buckie

Banff

Fraserburgh

North-east Scotland

North-east Scotland is dominated by high mountains. Here you can see reindeer, mountain hares, and birds and flowers that are usually only found in the Arctic. On the north and east coasts are important fishing towns. Aberdeen is the centre of the North Sea oil industry.

Crested Tit

Peterhead

Bagpipes
This musical instrument is played by blowing air into a bag, which is then squeezed out through various pipes. The melody is played on a pipe called a chanter.

Inverurie

RIVER DON

Cod

Crossbill
The unique beak of this rare bird enables it to peck seeds from pine and larch cones.

Aberdeen

RIVER DEE

Banchory

Balmoral Castle
Balmoral has been owned by the royal family since 1852. The Queen comes here every year on holiday.

Stonehaven

Dunnottar Castle

Fishing boat

Snow bunting

Montrose

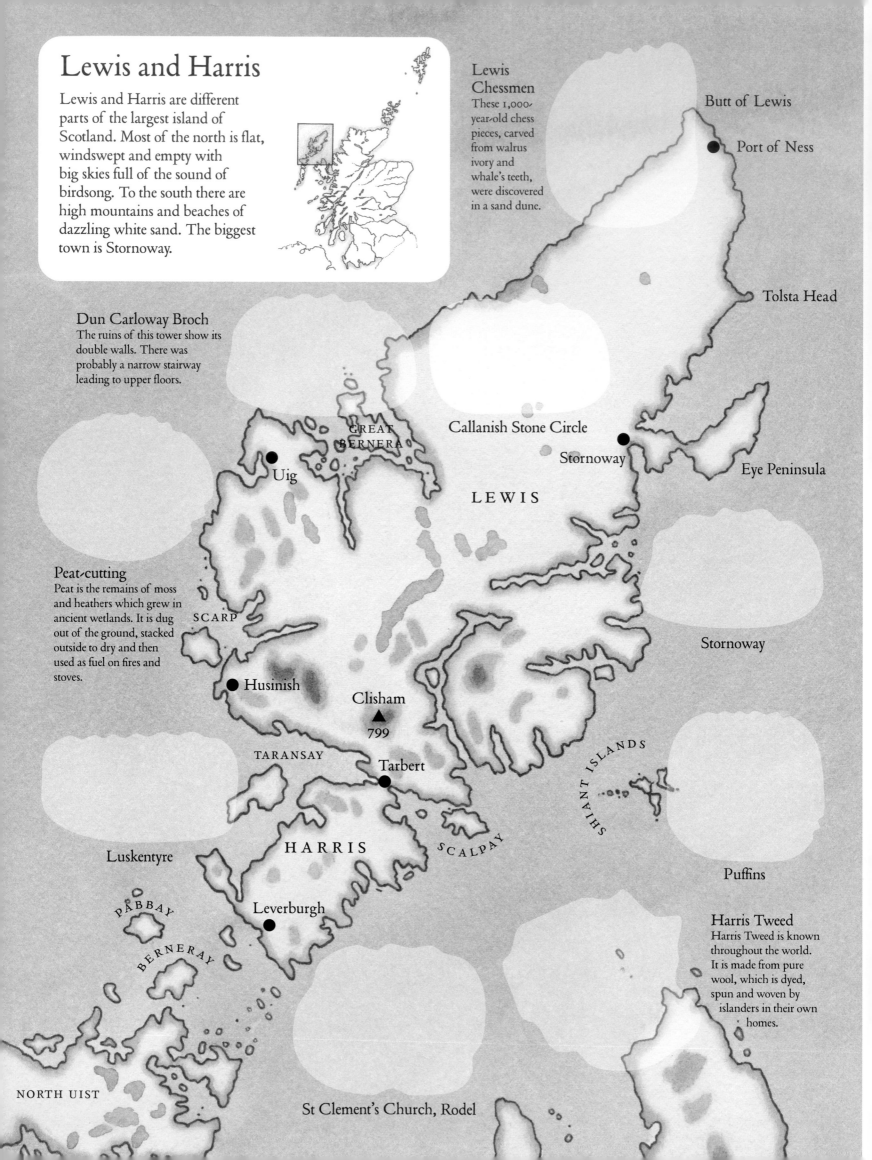

Lewis and Harris

Lewis and Harris are different parts of the largest island of Scotland. Most of the north is flat, windswept and empty with big skies full of the sound of birdsong. To the south there are high mountains and beaches of dazzling white sand. The biggest town is Stornoway.

Lewis Chessmen
These 1,000-year-old chess pieces, carved from walrus ivory and whale's teeth, were discovered in a sand dune.

Butt of Lewis

Port of Ness

Tolsta Head

Dun Carloway Broch
The ruins of this tower show its double walls. There was probably a narrow stairway leading to upper floors.

GREAT BERNERA

Callanish Stone Circle

Stornoway

Eye Peninsula

Uig

L E W I S

Peat-cutting
Peat is the remains of moss and heathers which grew in ancient wetlands. It is dug out of the ground, stacked outside to dry and then used as fuel on fires and stoves.

SCARP

Stornoway

Husinish

Clisham
▲
799

TARANSAY

Tarbert

SHIANT ISLANDS

Luskentyre

H A R R I S

SCALPAY

Puffins

PÀBBAY

Leverburgh

B E R N E R A Y

Harris Tweed
Harris Tweed is known throughout the world. It is made from pure wool, which is dyed, spun and woven by islanders in their own homes.

NORTH UIST

St Clement's Church, Rodel

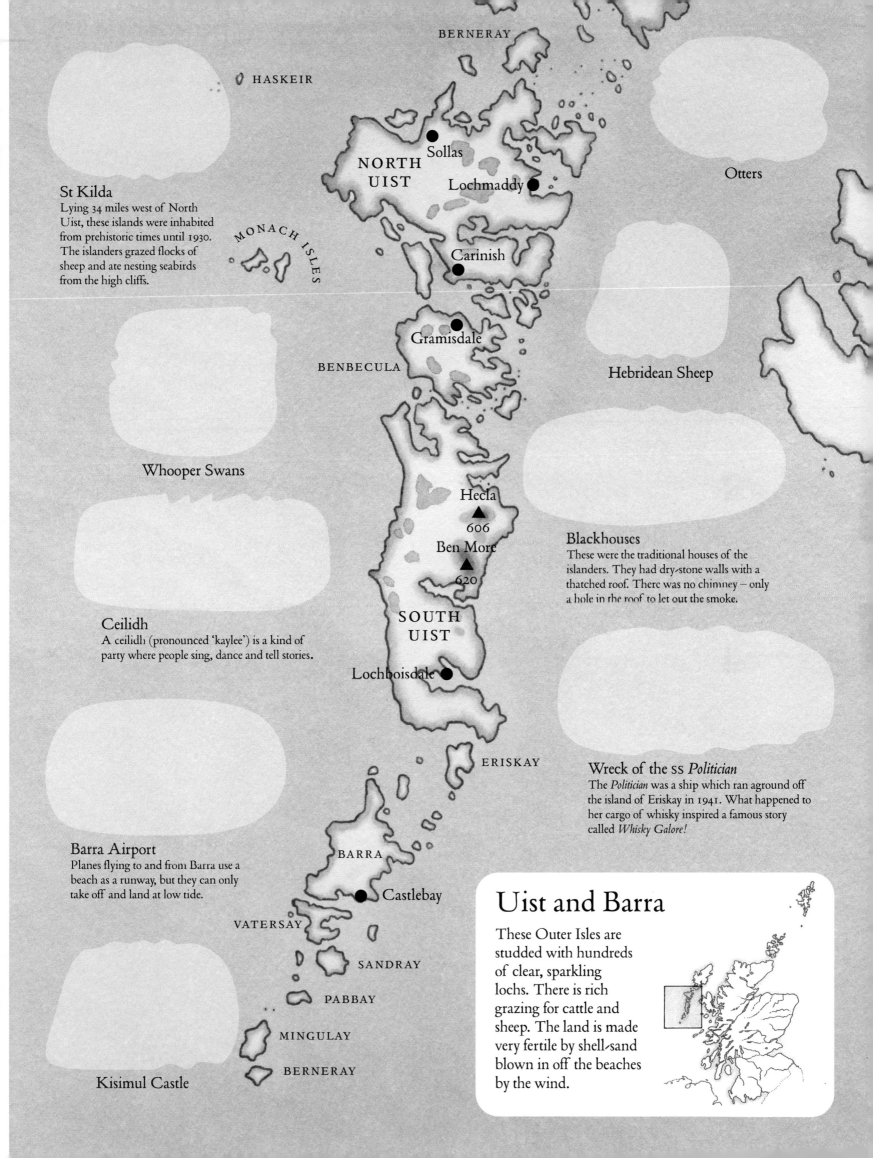

BERNERAY

HASKEIR

Sollas

NORTH
UIST

Lochmaddy

Otters

St Kilda
Lying 34 miles west of North
Uist, these islands were inhabited
from prehistoric times until 1930.
The islanders grazed flocks of
sheep and ate nesting seabirds
from the high cliffs.

MONACH ISLES

Carinish

Gramisdale

BENBECULA

Hebridean Sheep

Whooper Swans

Hecla
▲
606

Ben More
▲
620

Blackhouses
These were the traditional houses of the
islanders. They had dry-stone walls with a
thatched roof. There was no chimney – only
a hole in the roof to let out the smoke.

SOUTH
UIST

Ceilidh
A ceilidh (pronounced 'kaylee') is a kind of
party where people sing, dance and tell stories.

Lochboisdale

ERISKAY

Wreck of the ss *Politician*
The *Politician* was a ship which ran aground off
the island of Eriskay in 1941. What happened to
her cargo of whisky inspired a famous story
called *Whisky Galore!*

Barra Airport
Planes flying to and from Barra use a
beach as a runway, but they can only
take off and land at low tide.

BARRA

Castlebay

VATERSAY

SANDRAY

PABBAY

MINGULAY

BERNERAY

Kisimul Castle

Uist and Barra

These Outer Isles are
studded with hundreds
of clear, sparkling
lochs. There is rich
grazing for cattle and
sheep. The land is made
very fertile by shell-sand
blown in off the beaches
by the wind.

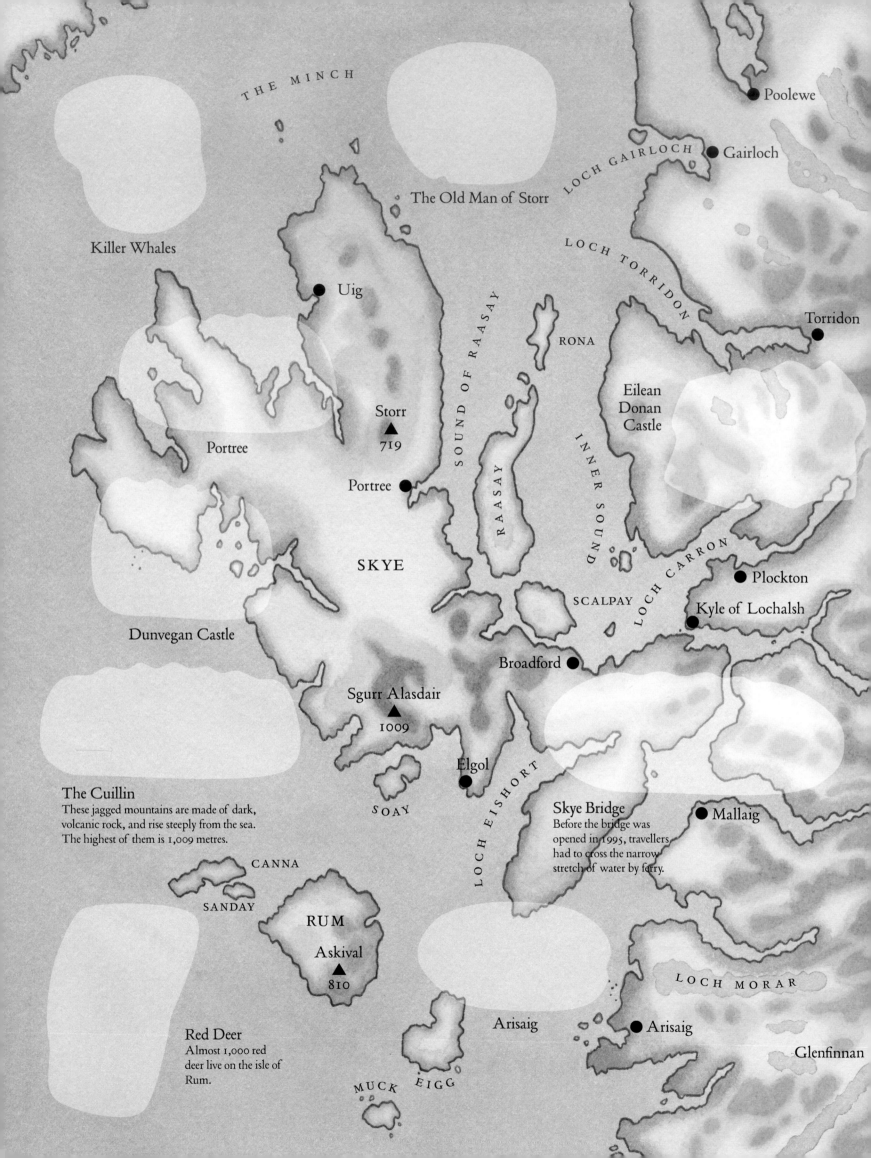

THE MINCH

Killer Whales

The Old Man of Storr

Poolewe

LOCH GAIRLOCH

Gairloch

LOCH TORRIDON

Torridon

Uig

SOUND OF RAASAY

RONA

Eilean
Donan
Castle

Storr
▲
719

Portree

RAASAY

INNER SOUND

Portree

SKYE

LOCH CARRON

Plockton

SCALPAY

Kyle of Lochalsh

Dunvegan Castle

Broadford

Sgurr Alasdair
▲
1009

Elgol

SOAY

LOCH EISHORT

Skye Bridge
Before the bridge was
opened in 1995, travellers
had to cross the narrow
stretch of water by ferry.

Mallaig

The Cuillin
These jagged mountains are made of dark,
volcanic rock, and rise steeply from the sea.
The highest of them is 1,009 metres.

CANNA

SANDAY

RUM

Askival
▲
810

LOCH MORAR

Red Deer
Almost 1,000 red
deer live on the isle of
Rum.

MUCK   EIGG

Arisaig

Arisaig

Glenfinnan

Skye and the Highlands

There are many islands off the west coast of Scotland. Skye is one of the biggest. On the mainland are long, deep lochs, dramatic glens and high mountains. This is the land of the otter, the golden eagle, the red deer and the wildcat. The town of Inverness is known as the capital of the Highlands.

Inverewe Gardens
Exotic plants from around the world grow along this stretch of coast because a warm ocean current (called the Gulf Stream) raises sea and air temperatures.

Caledonian Pine
These trees are direct descendants of the first pine forests that grew in Scotland after the last Ice Age.

Wildcat

Beauly ●   ● Inverness

LOCH MONAR   RIVER BEAULY

Sgurr na Lapaich
▲
1150

Carn Eige
▲
1182

GLEN AFFRIC

A' Chralaig
▲
1120

Pine Marten
A member of the otter, mink and badger family, the pine marten lives in woods and forests and is most active at night.

LOCH NESS

Shinty
This is a Highland team game played with a curved stick called a 'caman' and a hard ball.

Ptarmigan
The ptarmigan is the only British bird to dramatically change colour according to the season. In summer it is brown and in winter it is pure white.

Carn Ban
▲
941

● Fort Augustus

Glenfinnan Viaduct
This railway viaduct was completed in 1898 for the West Highland Line. It is 100 feet tall and has 21 arches or 'spans'.

Ice Climbing

Golden Eagle

● Fort William

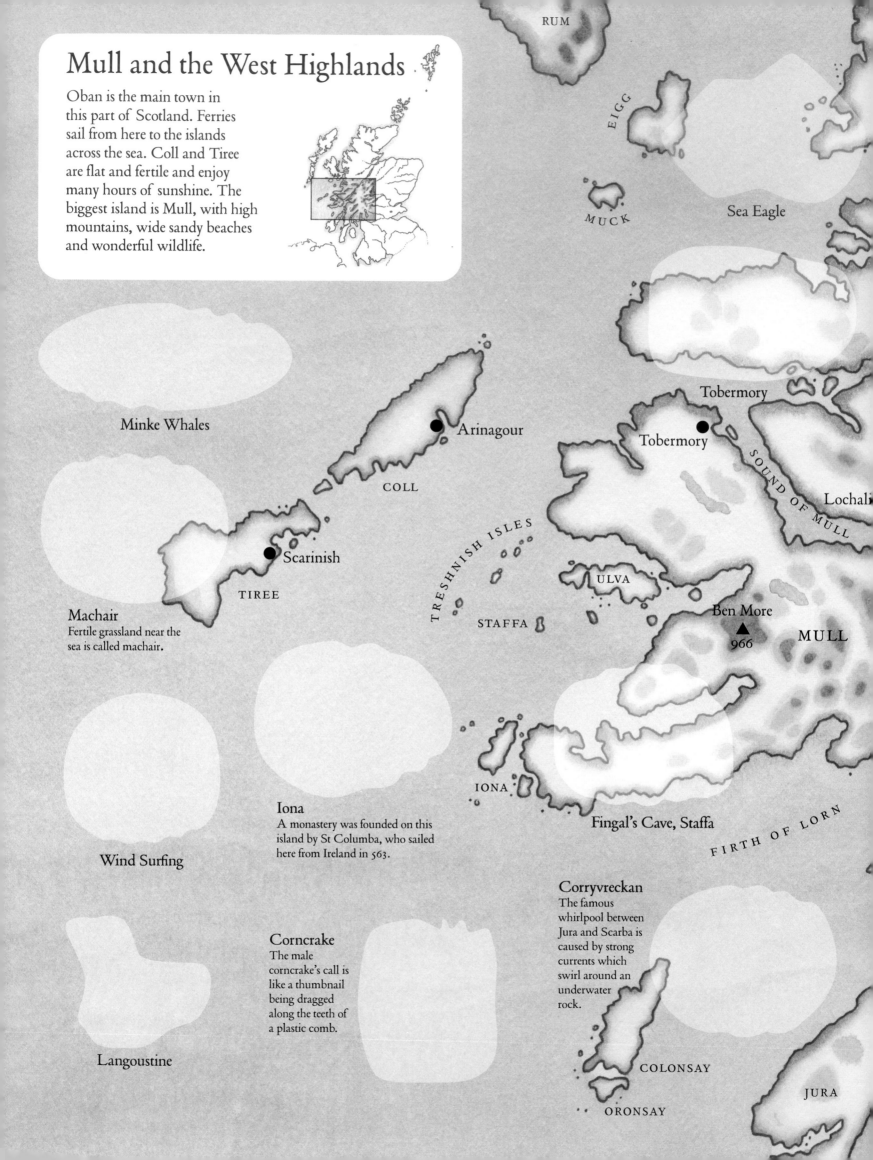

Mull and the West Highlands

Oban is the main town in this part of Scotland. Ferries sail from here to the islands across the sea. Coll and Tiree are flat and fertile and enjoy many hours of sunshine. The biggest island is Mull, with high mountains, wide sandy beaches and wonderful wildlife.

RUM

EIGG

MUCK

Sea Eagle

Tobermory

Tobermory

SOUND OF MULL

Lochali

Minke Whales

TRESHNISH ISLES

ULVA

Arinagour

COLL

Scarinish

TIREE

Machair
Fertile grassland near the sea is called machair.

STAFFA

Ben More
▲
966

MULL

IONA

Iona
A monastery was founded on this island by St Columba, who sailed here from Ireland in 563.

Fingal's Cave, Staffa

FIRTH OF LORN

Wind Surfing

Corryvreckan
The famous whirlpool between Jura and Scarba is caused by strong currents which swirl around an underwater rock.

Corncrake
The male corncrake's call is like a thumbnail being dragged along the teeth of a plastic comb.

Langoustine

COLONSAY

JURA

ORONSAY

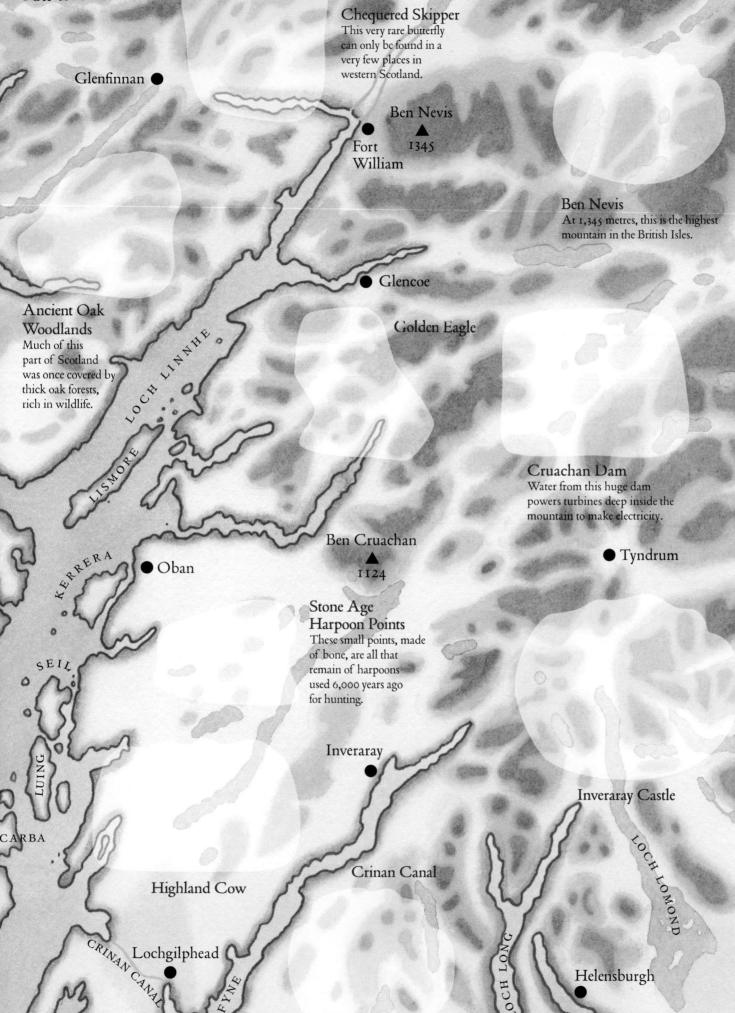

LOCH MORAR

Glenfinnan ●

Chequered Skipper
This very rare butterfly
can only be found in a
very few places in
western Scotland.

Ben Nevis
● ▲
Fort 1345
William

Ben Nevis
At 1,345 metres, this is the highest
mountain in the British Isles.

● Glencoe

LOCH LINNHE

**Ancient Oak
Woodlands**
Much of this
part of Scotland
was once covered by
thick oak forests,
rich in wildlife.

Golden Eagle

LISMORE

Cruachan Dam
Water from this huge dam
powers turbines deep inside the
mountain to make electricity.

Ben Cruachan
▲
1124

KERRERA

● Oban

● Tyndrum

**Stone Age
Harpoon Points**
These small points, made
of bone, are all that
remain of harpoons
used 6,000 years ago
for hunting.

SEIL

LUING

Inveraray
●

Inveraray Castle

LOCH LOMOND

SCARBA

Crinan Canal

Highland Cow

CRINAN CANAL

Lochgilphead
●

LOCH FYNE

LOCH LONG

Helensburgh
●

FIRTH OF CLYDE

LOCH ERICHT

Fife, Stirlingshire, Perthshire and Angus

Fife is one of the most historic parts of Scotland. North of Perthshire are the high, wild Grampian mountains. To the west is Loch Lomond – Scotland's most famous loch. The River Tay flows into the sea near Dundee, Scotland's fourth largest city.

Dalwhinnie

Whisky Distillery

LOCH RANNOCH

LOCH TU

Tossing the Caber
This event features in Highland Games and involves throwing a large tree trunk almost 20 feet long.

Ben Doran
▲
1074

LOCH TAY

Crannog
Crannogs were artificial islands on which a dwelling was built. The surrounding water gave safety from enemies and wild animals.

Capercaillie
The spectacular male capercaillie is a large, noisy and sometimes aggressive game bird found in pine forests.

Ben Lui
▲
1130

Crianlarich
●

Ben More
▲
1174

Lochearnhead
● LOCH EARN

Crieff ●

Birch tree

LOCH LOMOND

Red Squirrel

Stirling Castle

Stirling ●

The Stirling Torcs
In 2009 a valuable hoard of Iron Age treasure, including four gold necklaces, or 'torcs', was discovered in a field near Stirling.

Beinn à Ghlò
▲
1121

Glas Maol
▲
1067

GLEN SHEE

Aberdeen
Angus Cow

Blair Atholl

Brechin ●

Pitlochry ●

Red Grouse

Arbroath
Smokies
Haddock smoked
over a wood fire
is a speciality of
the fishing town
of Arbroath.

Snowboarding

Forfar ●

Blairgowric ●

Dunkeld ●

RIVER TAY

Raspberries
The land north of Perth is
perfect for growing raspberries,
strawberries and other soft fruit.

Arbroath ●

Dundee

FIRTH OF TAY

RRS *Discovery*
Launched in Dundee, this ship
was used by Ernest Shackleton and
Robert Scott on their famous
expedition to the Antarctic between
1901 and 1904.

Perth ●

St Andrews ●

Lochleven Castle
Mary, Queen of Scots was
imprisoned here in 1567.
After almost a year she
managed to escape in a
rowing boat, disguised
as a servant girl.

Crail ●

Bannockburn
In June 1314 at the
Battle of Bannockburn,
Robert the Bruce won
an important victory
over the English in the
struggle for Scottish
independence.

LOCH LEVEN

FIRTH OF FORTH

Kirkcaldy ●

Crail Harbour

Dunfermline ●

North
Queensferry

Inchcolm
The abbey on this island is
dedicated to St Columba,
a Christian missionary
from Iona who is said to
have visited here in 567.

Edinburgh ●

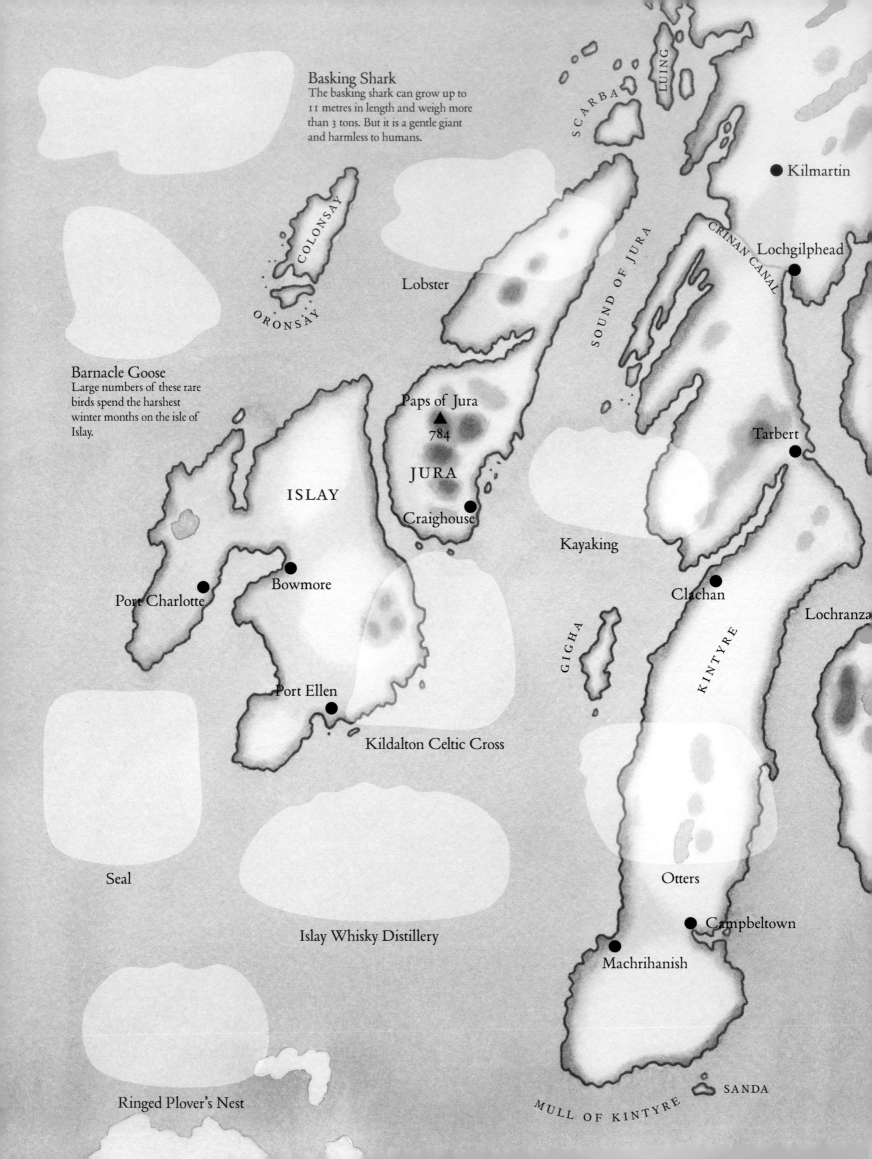

Basking Shark
The basking shark can grow up to 11 metres in length and weigh more than 3 tons. But it is a gentle giant and harmless to humans.

Barnacle Goose
Large numbers of these rare birds spend the harshest winter months on the isle of Islay.

SCARBA

LUING

COLONSAY

ORONSAY

Lobster

• Kilmartin

SOUND OF JURA

CRINAN CANAL

Lochgilphead •

Paps of Jura
▲
784

JURA

Tarbert
•

ISLAY

Craighouse •

Kayaking

Port Charlotte
•

Bowmore
•

GIGHA

Clachan
•

KINTYRE

Lochranza

Port Ellen
•

Kildalton Celtic Cross

Seal

Otters

Campbeltown
•

Islay Whisky Distillery

Machrihanish
•

Ringed Plover's Nest

SANDA

MULL OF KINTYRE

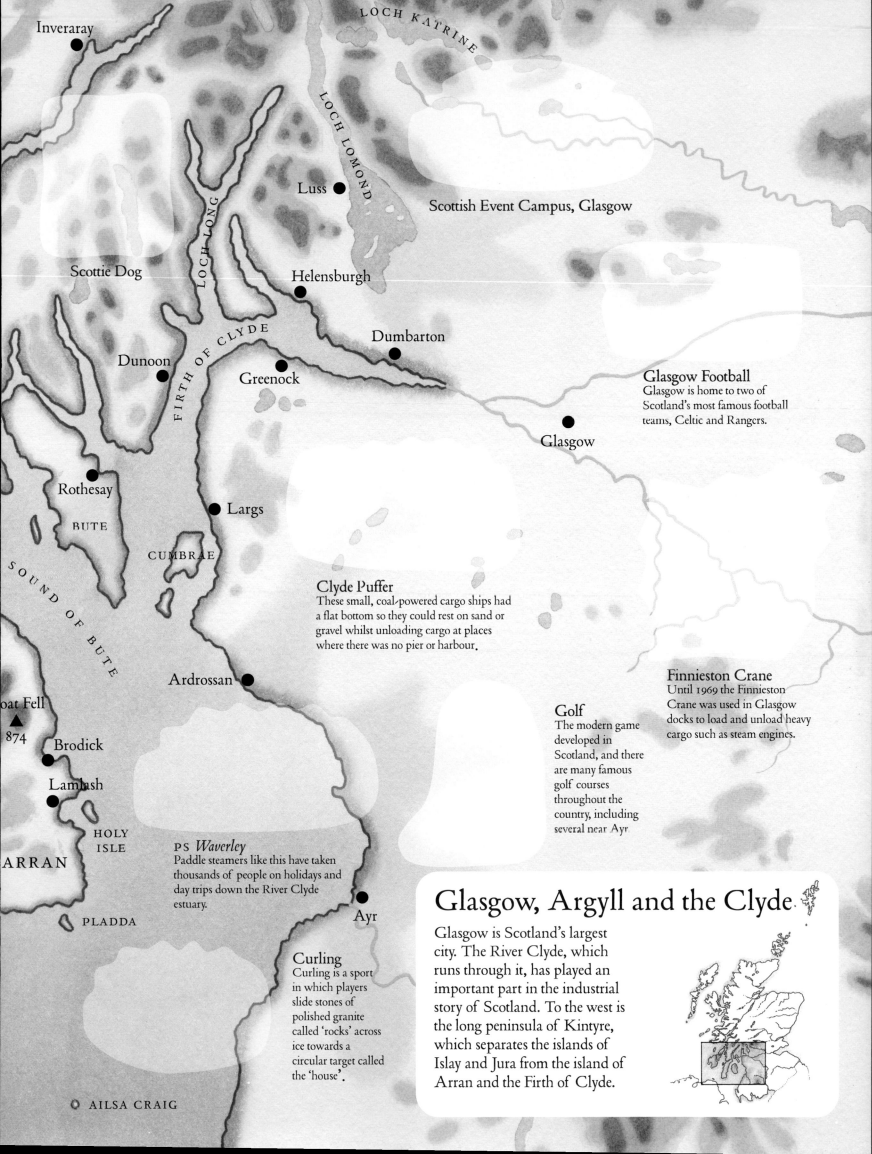

Inveraray

LOCH KATRINE

LOCH LOMOND

Luss

Scottish Event Campus, Glasgow

LOCH LONG

Scottie Dog

Helensburgh

Dumbarton

FIRTH OF CLYDE

Dunoon

Greenock

Glasgow Football
Glasgow is home to two of
Scotland's most famous football
teams, Celtic and Rangers.

Glasgow

Rothesay

Largs

BUTE

CUMBRAE

Clyde Puffer
These small, coal-powered cargo ships had
a flat bottom so they could rest on sand or
gravel whilst unloading cargo at places
where there was no pier or harbour.

SOUND OF BUTE

Ardrossan

Finnieston Crane
Until 1969 the Finnieston
Crane was used in Glasgow
docks to load and unload heavy
cargo such as steam engines.

oat Fell
▲
874

Brodick

Golf
The modern game
developed in
Scotland, and there
are many famous
golf courses
throughout the
country, including
several near Ayr.

Lamlash

HOLY
ISLE

ARRAN

PS *Waverley*
Paddle steamers like this have taken
thousands of people on holidays and
day trips down the River Clyde
estuary.

PLADDA

Ayr

Curling
Curling is a sport
in which players
slide stones of
polished granite
called 'rocks' across
ice towards a
circular target called
the 'house'.

Glasgow, Argyll and the Clyde

Glasgow is Scotland's largest
city. The River Clyde, which
runs through it, has played an
important part in the industrial
story of Scotland. To the west is
the long peninsula of Kintyre,
which separates the islands of
Islay and Jura from the island of
Arran and the Firth of Clyde.

○ AILSA CRAIG

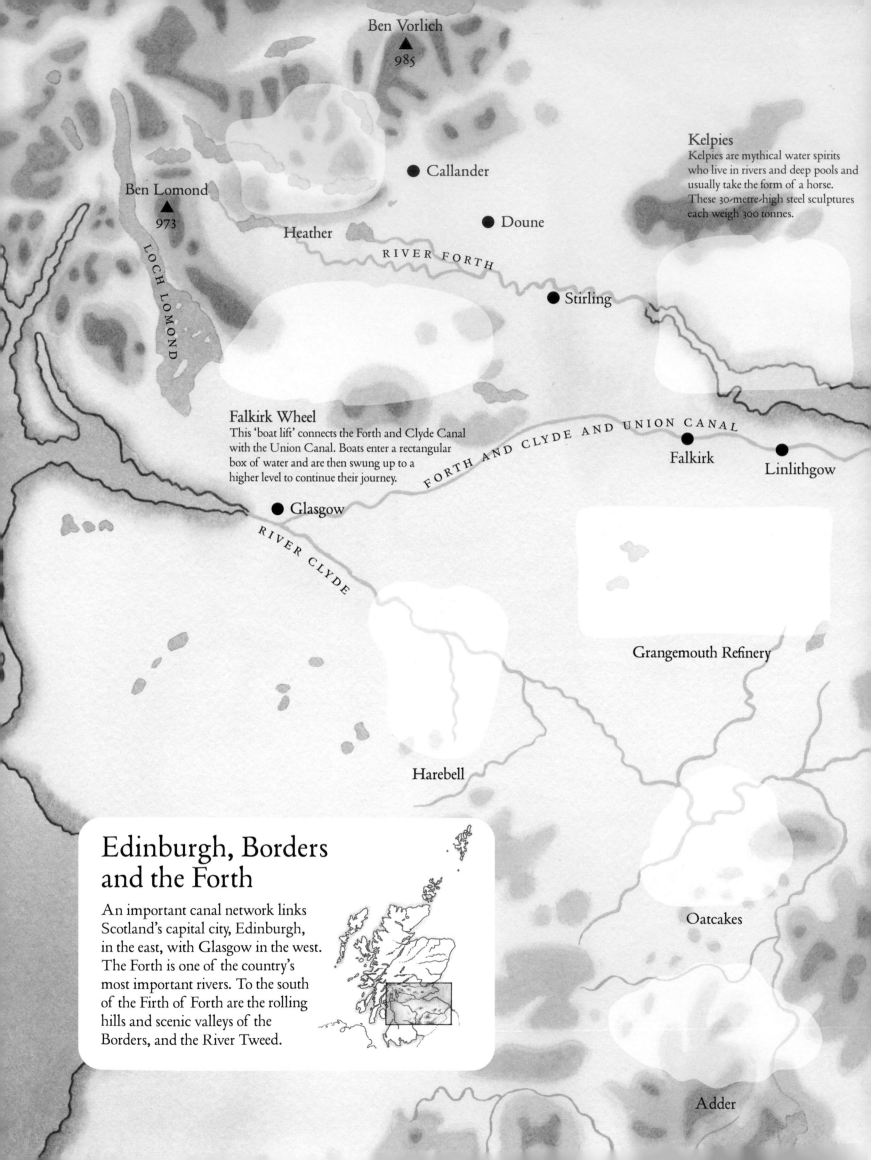

Ben Vorlich ▲
985

Kelpies
Kelpies are mythical water spirits who live in rivers and deep pools and usually take the form of a horse. These 30-metre-high steel sculptures each weigh 300 tonnes.

● Callander

Ben Lomond ▲
973

● Doune

Heather

RIVER FORTH

LOCH LOMOND

● Stirling

Falkirk Wheel
This 'boat lift' connects the Forth and Clyde Canal with the Union Canal. Boats enter a rectangular box of water and are then swung up to a higher level to continue their journey.

FORTH AND CLYDE AND UNION CANAL

● Falkirk

● Linlithgow

● Glasgow

RIVER CLYDE

Grangemouth Refinery

Harebell

Edinburgh, Borders and the Forth

An important canal network links Scotland's capital city, Edinburgh, in the east, with Glasgow in the west. The Forth is one of the country's most important rivers. To the south of the Firth of Forth are the rolling hills and scenic valleys of the Borders, and the River Tweed.

Oatcakes

Adder

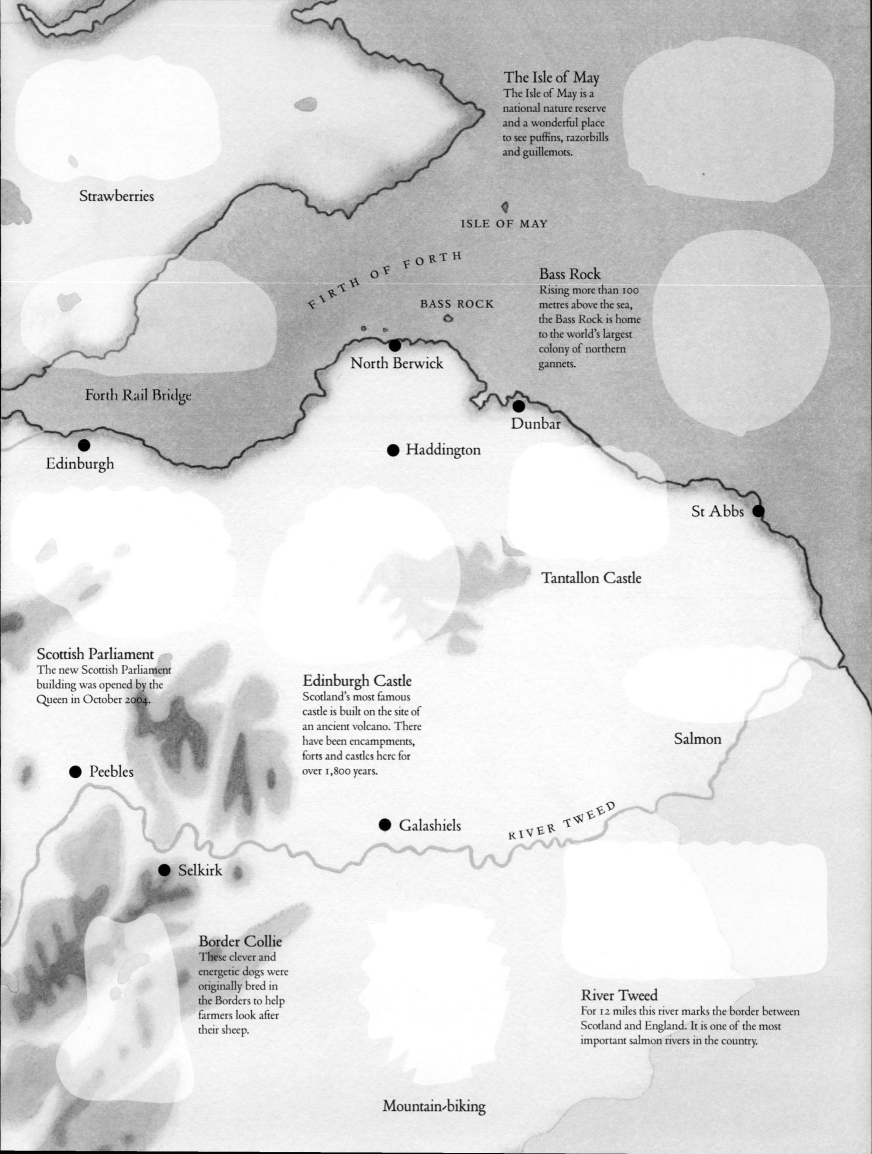

The Isle of May
The Isle of May is a national nature reserve and a wonderful place to see puffins, razorbills and guillemots.

Strawberries

ISLE OF MAY

FIRTH OF FORTH

BASS ROCK

Bass Rock
Rising more than 100 metres above the sea, the Bass Rock is home to the world's largest colony of northern gannets.

North Berwick

Forth Rail Bridge

Dunbar

Edinburgh

Haddington

St Abbs

Tantallon Castle

Scottish Parliament
The new Scottish Parliament building was opened by the Queen in October 2004.

Edinburgh Castle
Scotland's most famous castle is built on the site of an ancient volcano. There have been encampments, forts and castles here for over 1,800 years.

Salmon

Peebles

Galashiels

RIVER TWEED

Selkirk

Border Collie
These clever and energetic dogs were originally bred in the Borders to help farmers look after their sheep.

River Tweed
For 12 miles this river marks the border between Scotland and England. It is one of the most important salmon rivers in the country.

Mountain-biking

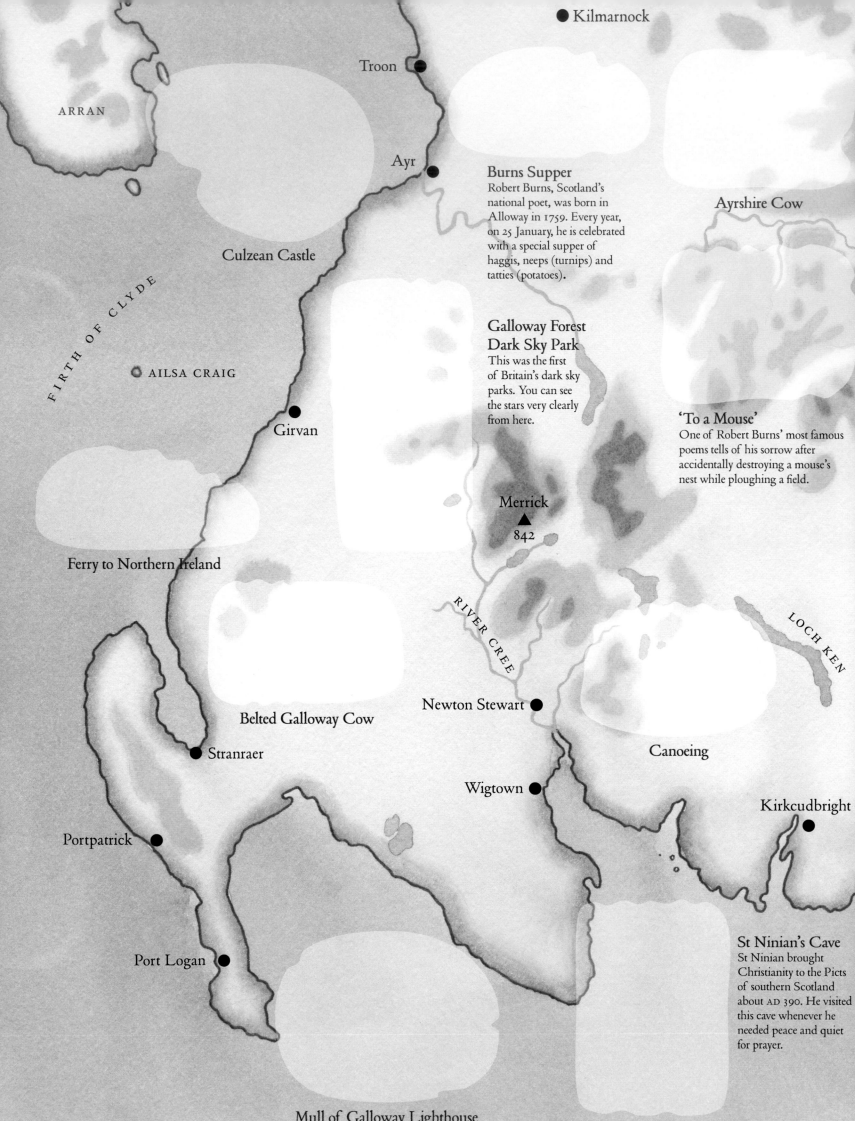

Kilmarnock

Troon

ARRAN

Ayr

Burns Supper
Robert Burns, Scotland's
national poet, was born in
Alloway in 1759. Every year,
on 25 January, he is celebrated
with a special supper of
haggis, neeps (turnips) and
tatties (potatoes).

Ayrshire Cow

Culzean Castle

FIRTH OF CLYDE

**Galloway Forest
Dark Sky Park**
This was the first
of Britain's dark sky
parks. You can see
the stars very clearly
from here.

AILSA CRAIG

'To a Mouse'
One of Robert Burns' most famous
poems tells of his sorrow after
accidentally destroying a mouse's
nest while ploughing a field.

Girvan

Merrick
▲
842

Ferry to Northern Ireland

RIVER CREE

LOCH KEN

Belted Galloway Cow

Newton Stewart

Canoeing

Stranraer

Wigtown

Kirkcudbright

Portpatrick

Port Logan

St Ninian's Cave
St Ninian brought
Christianity to the Picts
of southern Scotland
about AD 390. He visited
this cave whenever he
needed peace and quiet
for prayer.

Mull of Galloway Lighthouse

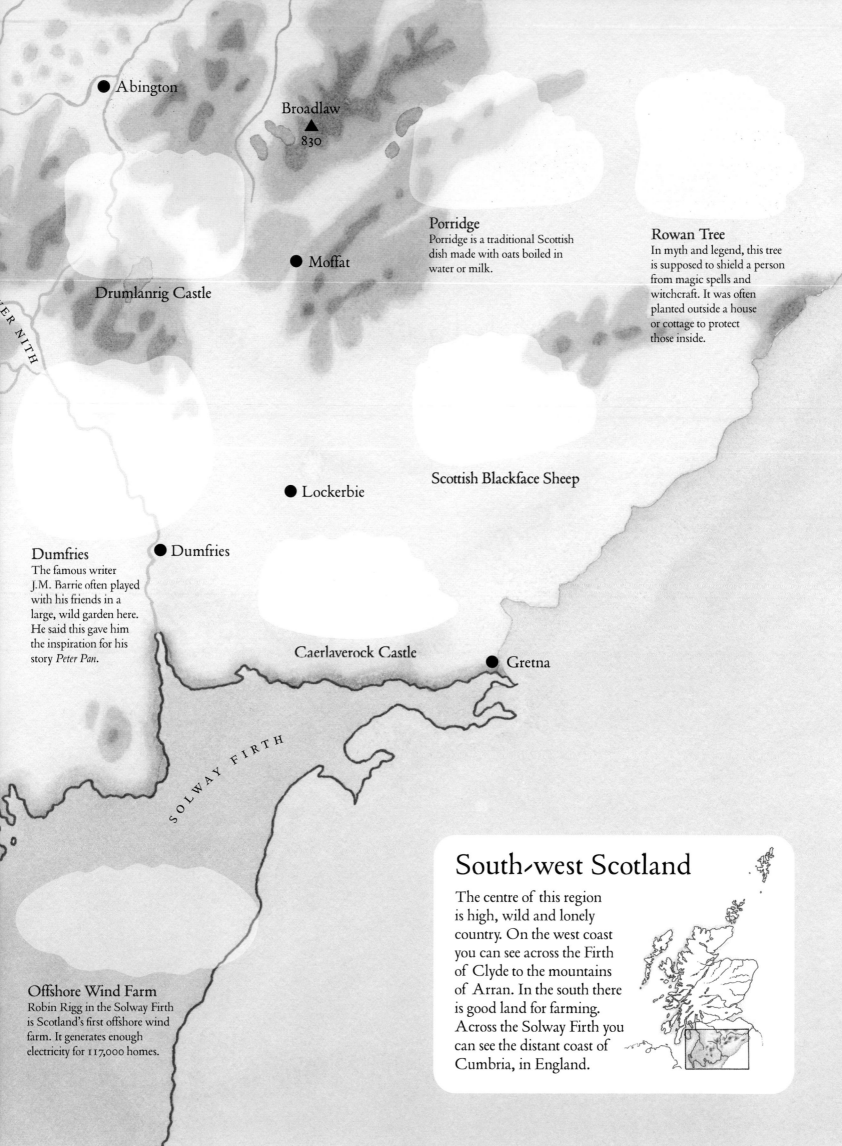

● Abington

Broadlaw
▲
830

● Moffat

Drumlanrig Castle

Porridge
Porridge is a traditional Scottish dish made with oats boiled in water or milk.

Rowan Tree
In myth and legend, this tree is supposed to shield a person from magic spells and witchcraft. It was often planted outside a house or cottage to protect those inside.

ER NITH

Scottish Blackface Sheep

● Lockerbie

Dumfries
The famous writer J.M. Barrie often played with his friends in a large, wild garden here. He said this gave him the inspiration for his story *Peter Pan*.

● Dumfries

Caerlaverock Castle

● Gretna

SOLWAY FIRTH

Offshore Wind Farm
Robin Rigg in the Solway Firth is Scotland's first offshore wind farm. It generates enough electricity for 117,000 homes.

South-west Scotland

The centre of this region is high, wild and lonely country. On the west coast you can see across the Firth of Clyde to the mountains of Arran. In the south there is good land for farming. Across the Solway Firth you can see the distant coast of Cumbria, in England.

Quiz

Can you find? . . .

The highest mountain in Britain? (Clue: It's in the West Highlands)

An island on which a large number of red deer live? (Clue: Look for it near the isle of Skye)

A special 'boat lift'? (Clue: It connects two canals between Edinburgh and Glasgow)

A place where you can see the stars very clearly? (Clue: Look for it in south-west Scotland)

A city with two famous football teams? (Clue: It's in the west of Scotland)

A place where thousands of birds make their nests? (Clue: It's off the north-west coast of Scotland)

An airport where the runway is on a beach? (Clue: Look for it on an island off the west coast of Scotland)

A village where people lived thousands of years ago? (Clue: It's on a group of islands very far north)

The castle where the Queen goes on holiday every year? (Clue: It's west of Aberdeen)

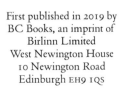

The site of a famous battle which was fought in 1314? (Clue: It took place near Stirling)

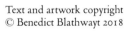

A famous monster that lives in a loch? (Clue: You'll find it near Inverness)

A bird which changes its colour according to the season? (Clue: It lives in the high mountains of the Highlands)

For Georgina, Charlie, Phoebe and Alec

First published in 2019 by BC Books, an imprint of Birlinn Limited West Newington House 10 Newington Road Edinburgh EH9 1QS

www.bcbooksforkids.co.uk

Text and artwork copyright © Benedict Blathwayt 2018

ISBN: 978 1 78027 412 6

Designed by Mark Blackadder

Printed and bound in China

Shetland and Orkney stickers

Viking Boat

Ring of Brodgar

St Magnus Cathedral, Kirkwall

Mousa Boch

Sullom Voe Refinery

Up Helly Aa

Ferry to Orkney

Grey Seals

Fair Isle Jumper

Skara Brae

Shetland Pony

The Old Man of Hoy

North Ronaldsay Beacon

Snowy Owl

Arctic Skua

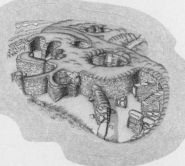

Jarlshof

Lerwick

Northern Scotland stickers

Aurora Borealis

Pictish Stone Carving

Great Stack of Handa

Keiss Castle

Surfing

Rock Climbing

Suilven

Duncansby Stacks

Curlew

Oil rig

Summer Isles

Sandwood Bay

Ardvreck Castle

Heather

Primula Scotica

Grey Cairns of Camster

Ferry to Stornoway

Great Northern Diver

North-east Scotland stickers

Skiing

Gentian

Reindeer

Bagpipes

Dunnottar Castle

Urquhart Castle

Fishing boat

Crested Tit

Whisky

Mountain hare

Osprey

Dolphins

Loch Ness Monster

Balmoral Castle

Cod

Snow bunting

Crossbill

Battle of Culloden

Lewis and Harris, Uist and Barra stickers

Puffins

Hebridean Sheep

Harris Tweed

Lewis Chessmen

Ceilidh

Blackhouses

Stornoway

Callanish Stone Circle

Wreck of the ss *Politician*

Luskentyre

Barra Airport

Dun Carloway
Broch

Kisimul Castle

St Kilda

Peat-cutting

St Clement's Church, Rodel

Otters

Whooper Swans

Skye and the Highlands stickers

Eilean Donan Castle

Golden Eagle

Caledonian Pine

Ice Climbing

Red Deer

Wildcat

Glenfinnan Viaduct

Killer Whales

Ptarmigan

Skye Bridge

Arisaig

Dunvegan Castle

The Cuillin

Portree

Inverewe Gardens

Shinty

Pine Marten

The Old Man of Storr

Mull and the West Highlands stickers

Chequered Skipper

Machair

Corncrake

Inveraray Castle

Ancient Oak Woodlands

Ben Nevis

Cruachan Dam

Wind Surfing

Iona

Langoustine

Stone Age Harpoon Points

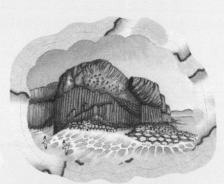

Fingal's Cave, Staffa

Highland Cow

Tobermory

Minke Whales

Golden Eagle

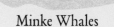

Sea Eagle

Crinan Canal

Corryvreckan

Fife, Stirlingshire, Perthshire and Angus stickers

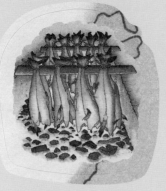

Arbroath Smokies

Snowboarding

Red Grouse

Bannockburn

Whisky Distillery

Red Squirrel

Capercaillie

Crail Harbour

Aberdeen Angus Cow

Lochleven Castle

The Stirling Torcs

Stirling Castle

Raspberries

Birch tree

Crannog

Inchcolm

RRS *Discovery*

Tossing the Caber

Glasgow, Argyll and the Clyde stickers

Seal

Golf

Kildalton Celtic Cross

Finnieston Crane

Otters

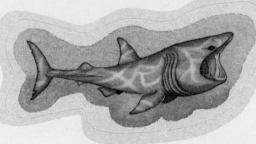

Basking Shark

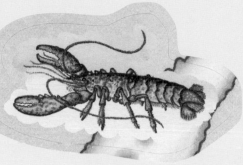

Lobster

Barnacle Goose

Ringed Plover's Nest

Scottie Dog

Curling

Scottish Event Campus, Glasgow

Glasgow Football

Clyde Puffer

Islay Whisky Distillery

Kayaking

PS *Waverley*

Edinburgh, Borders and the Forth stickers

Scottish Parliament

Harebell

Border Collie

Bass Rock

Forth Rail Bridge

Tantallon Castle

Falkirk Wheel

Kelpies

The Isle of May

River Tweed

Salmon

Edinburgh Castle

Mountain-biking

Oatcakes

Heather

Adder

Strawberries

Grangemouth Refinery

South-west Scotland stickers

Offshore Wind Farm

Ferry to Northern Ireland

Porridge

Belted Galloway Cow

Ayrshire Cow

Canocing

Burns Supper

Culzean Castle

Mull of Galloway Lighthouse

Caerlaverock Castle

Scottish Blackface
Sheep

Drumlanrig Castle

Dumfries

'To a Mouse'

Rowan Tree

St Ninian's Cave

Galloway Forest
Dark Sky Park